SAM

DAN

With thanks to
Virginia Lee Burton
without whom I might not
have read a book. L.H.

Random House Children's Books

Published by Random House Children's Books
20 Vauxhall Bridge Road, London SW1V 2SA

A division of Random House UK Ltd
London Melbourne Sydney Auckland
Johannesburg and agencies throughout the world

Copyright © Laurence Hutchins 1996

1 3 5 7 9 10 8 6 4 2

First published by Random House Children's Books 1996

Printed in Singapore

RANDOM HOUSE UK Limited Reg. No. 954009

ISBN 0 09 968201 X

NERO

— Laurence Hutchins —

Random House 🏠 Children's Books

Nero was lonely, shut up in his shed.

Nobody came to see him any more –

not even Driver Jones. Then one day the door opened...

"It's a steam engine," said Sam

"Let's clean him up," said Dan.

So they cleared Nero's chimney,

and washed his tank,

and polished the dome,

and cleaned the cab.

Nero looked like new!
And then the door opened again.

It was Driver Jones.

"We've cleaned Nero up," said Sam and Dan.

"And a wonderful job you've done," said Driver Jones. "I haven't been able to look after Nero like that for a long time."

"Does he still go?" said Sam.

"Let's find out,"
said Driver Jones.

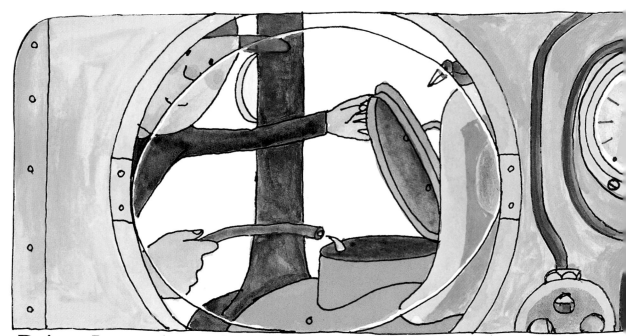

Driver Jones showed Dan how to put water into Nero's tank.
He showed Sam how to oil Nero's wheels.

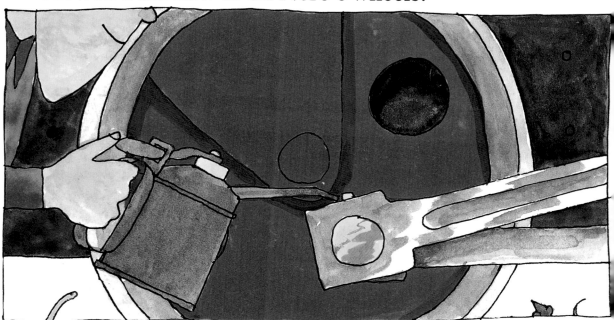

Then Driver Jones shovelled coal into Nero's firebox
and lit the fire.

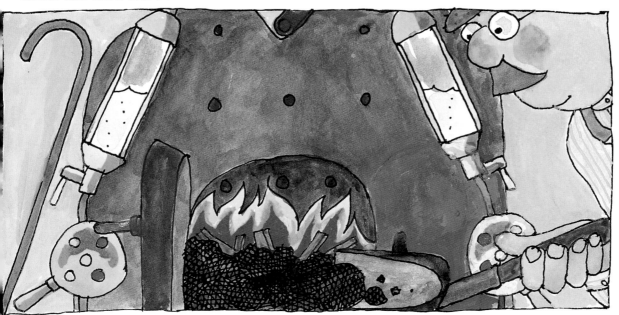

Nero built up steam, and Driver Jones blew the whistle.

"He *will* go! He *will* go!" shouted Sam and Dan. "Everyone will be so pleased to see Nero working again."

But when thick smoke was seen billowing from Nero's hut, no-one was pleased at all!

"Fire! Fire!" everyone shouted. "Quick, we must save Nero!"

So the plumber, the butcher, the postman, the school teacher, all the children and their mothers and fathers, rushed to save Nero.

Nero gave an extra burst of steam.

"Nero's not on fire. He's working!" Shouted Sam and Dan.

Everyone cheered.

And Nero was never
lonely again.

SAM

DAN